Written by David Bedford
Illustrated by Brenna Vaughan and Henry St. Leger

First published 2013 by Parragon Books, Ltd.
Copyright © 2018 Cottage Door Press, LLC
5005 Newport Drive, Rolling Meadows, Illinois 60008
All Rights Reserved

10 9 8 7 6 5 4 3 2 1

ISBN 978-1-68052-539-7

Parragon Books is an imprint of Cottage Door Press, LLC.
Parragon Books® and the Parragon® logo are
registered trademarks of Cottage Door Press, LLC.

I love my Daddy

PaRRagon.

One day, Little Squirrel went out to play with
his daddy. Little Squirrel wanted to show
Daddy Squirrel all the things he could do.

"What should we play first?" asked Daddy.

"I know," said Little Squirrel
excitedly …

"Digging!
Look, Daddy!" said Little Squirrel,

as he dug
and dug
and dug,

with his little
tail wagging.

"Good job!" said Daddy.
But suddenly, Little Squirrel's
tail stopped wagging.

"Help, Daddy!" cried Little Squirrel. "I'm stuck!"

Daddy Squirrel helped Little
Squirrel wriggle out of the hole,
and gave him a soothing hug. "You
are a good digger!" said Daddy.

"What should we play next?"

"I know," said Little Squirrel …

"Climbing!

Look, Daddy!" said Little Squirrel, and he climbed as high as he could go, looking around as far as he could see.

"Good job!" said Daddy.
But suddenly Little Squirrel
closed his eyes tightly …

"Help, Daddy!"

cried Little Squirrel.

"I'm stuck!"

Daddy Squirrel helped Little Squirrel climb down and gave him a soothing hug. "You are a good climber!" said Daddy. "What should we play next?"

"I know ...

Jumping!

Look, Daddy!" said Little Squirrel,

and he jumped

and jumped

and JUMPED,

with a big smile on his
little squirrel face.

But suddenly Little Squirrel
stopped smiling, and …

Splat!

"Help, Daddy!" cried Little
Squirrel. "I'm stuck again!"

Daddy Squirrel helped Little
Squirrel out of the sticky mud and
gave him a soothing hug.

"You are good
at jumping!" said Daddy.
But Little Squirrel shook
his head sadly …

"I don't want to play anymore,"
said Little Squirrel.

"I always get stuck.
I can't do anything!"

Daddy Squirrel lifted Little
Squirrel high onto his shoulders.
"Let's play together," he said.

"Let's run!"
cried Daddy Squirrel.

Little Squirrel held on
tightly as they whooshed
through the woods.

"Yippeee!"
he shouted.

"Let's climb!"
said Daddy Squirrel.
Little Squirrel kept his eyes
open wide as they reached
the top of a tree.

"Wheeee!" he shouted.

"And now," said Daddy Squirrel,

"let's jump!"

Splat!

"Oh, help!"
cried Daddy Squirrel.
"Now I'm stuck!"

Little Squirrel
giggled as he helped
his daddy out of the
sticky mud.

"You can do **everything**, Little Squirrel!" said Daddy proudly, as they washed their muddy paws in the stream. "You can even save a Daddy Squirrel!"

Little Squirrel climbed high onto his daddy's shoulders again. "I love playing with you, Daddy," he said. "And …"

"I love my daddy!"

shouted Little Squirrel,
as they raced home
happily together.